I
Am
Six

Published by Silver Press,
an imprint of Silver Burdett Press,
A Simon & Schuster Company
299 Jefferson Road, Parsippany, NJ 07054

Designed by Marie Fitzgerald
Finger paintings by Daniel Brooks and Mark Tobia

Manufactured in the United States of America

10 9 8 7 6 5 4 3 2 1

Library of Congress Cataloging-in-Publication Data
Morris, Ann, 1930-
    I Am Six/By Ann Morris: illustrated by Nancy
Sheehan.   p. cm.
    Summary: Photographs and brief text depict
what school is like for a six-year old.
    (1. Schools—fiction.)   I. Sheehan, Nancy, ill.
II. Title.   PZ7.M82724Iaac   1995
(E)—dc20   94-30495   CIP   AC
ISBN 0-382-24686-1 (JHC)   ISBN 0-382-24759-0 (LSB)
ISBN 0-382-24688-8 (S/C)

I Am Six

by Ann Morris

photographs by Nancy Sheehan

Silver Press

Parsippany, New Jersey

We wish to thank the staff and children of the Manhattan New School for their help in creating this book, especially master teacher Carmen Colon and her class and Principal Shelley Harwayne. Without their support, cooperation, and imagination, this book would not have been possible.

Ann Morris ● *Nancy Sheehan*

I am six.

I am six.

I am six.

We are six.

We are all six.

Here is our class.

Here is our teacher.

Here is our school.

Our snake,

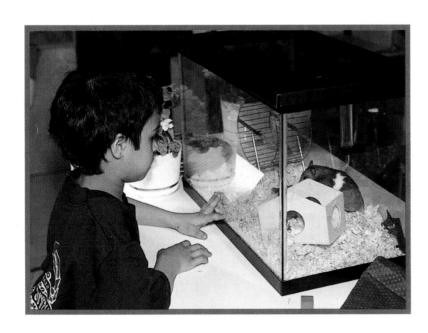

our hamster,

our mouse,
all live at school.

We read.

We write.

We count.

We sing.

We paint.

We play every day.

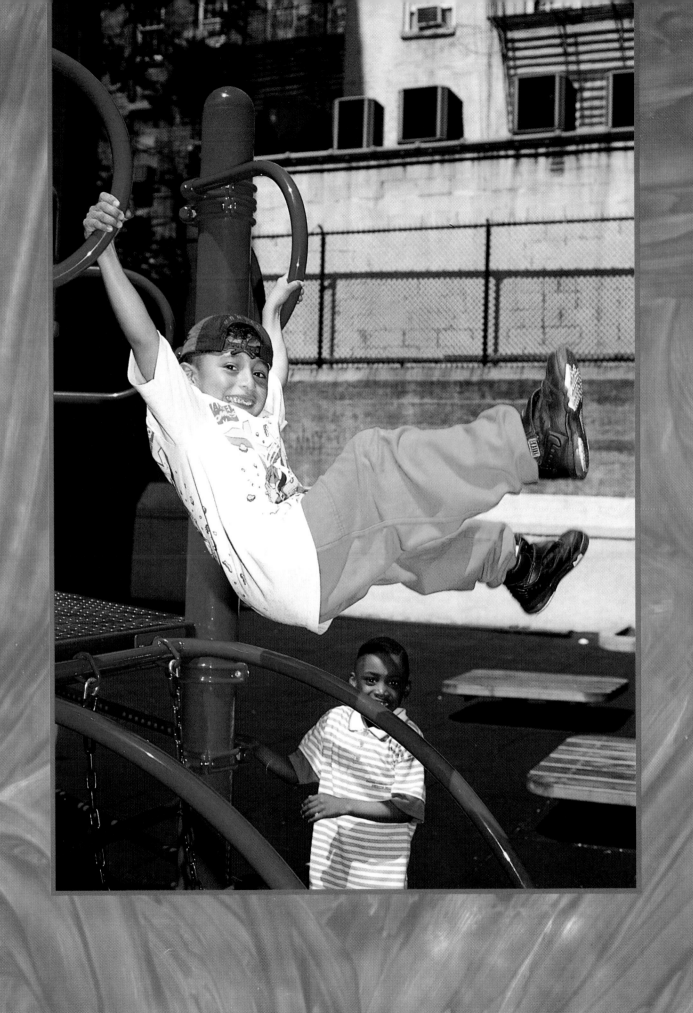

We walk.

We talk.

We wiggle.
We giggle.

We make friends.

We go to the zoo.

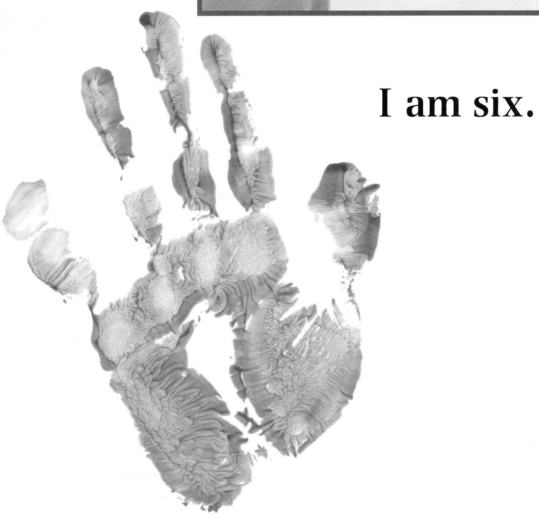

I am six.

We are all six!

© Paul Kolnik

Ann Morris

Ann Morris's many books for children include *Bread Bread Bread, Hats Hats Hats, How Teddy Bears Are Made,* and *Dancing to America.* She has been a teacher in public and private schools and has taught courses in language arts, children's literature, and writing for children at Bank Street College, Teachers College, and Queens College of the City University of New York, and at The New School in New York City.

© Paul Krashefski

Nancy Sheehan

Nancy Sheehan's special love is photographing children and animals. Her photos appear in major magazines, schoolbooks, and trade books. A former teacher who has worked extensively with children of all ages, Nancy and her sheep Molly live in Gloucester, Massachusetts.

73 CRIME & DETECTION

74 RUSSIA

75 LIGHT

76 ENERGY

77 ELECTRICITY

81 TIME & SPACE

82 ASTRONOMY

83 EARTH

84 LIFE

85 EVOLUTION

86 ECOLOGY

87 HUMAN BODY

88 MEDICINE

89 TECHNOLOGY

90 ELECTRONICS

RENAISSANCE

95 MONET

96 VAN GOGH

97 WATERCOLOR

98 PERSPECTIVE

DANCE

103 OLYMPICS

104 MEDIA & COMMUNICATION

105 TITANIC

106 FOOTBALL

HURRICANE & TORNADO

111 EPIDEMIC

112 WORLD WAR II

113 SUPER BOWL

114 CIVIL WAR

119 SHAKESPEARE

120 WILD WEST

121 AMERICAN REVOLUTION

122 INDIA

ISLAM

127 BASKETBALL

128 BUDDHISM

129 SUBMARINE